The Little Ghost Who Lost Her BOO!

Words by Elaine Bickell

Illustrations by Raymond McGrath

PHILOMEL

PHILOMEL BOOKS

An imprint of Penguin Random House LLC, New York

First published in the United States of America by Philomel, an imprint of Penguin Random House LLC, 2020.

First published in New Zealand by Scholastic New Zealand, 2019.

Text copyright © 2019 by Elaine Bickell.
Illustrations copyright © 2019 by Raymond McGrath.

Philomel Books is a registered trademark of Penguin Random House LLC.

Visit us online at penguinrandomhouse.com

Library of Congress Cataloging-in-Publication Data is available.

Manufactured in China.

ISBN 9780593202159

10 9 8 7 6 5 4 3 2 1

U.S. edition edited by Cheryl Eissing.
U.S. edition designed by Ellice Lee.
Text set in 18.5/33-point Just Tell Me What.

For Max, Gus, and Greta — E.B.

Come on now, it's up to you.

Let me hear you shout out,

"BOO!"

BOO!

Yes, that's it! That will do.
That is such a **SCARY BOO!**

You did it! You found it.
High-five, and a big **thank-you.**

And with that wonderful, scary boo,
away that happy Little Ghost flew.

She saw the reader!
Yes! She saw YOU!
Can **you** help Little Ghost find her **BOO?**

So Little Ghost went home, as sad as can be.

Then she looked up . . . and what did she see?

"It's close," said Little Ghost, "but it just won't do.
Even though it's similar, and perfect for you,
it's just not as scary as my own **GHOSTLY BOO**."

"Oh, hello, Cow, of course it's you.

I wonder, can you help me? I'm looking for my **BOO**."

"I'm sorry, Little Ghost, but I can't help you.

After being milked, I found some grass to chew,

but not once this morning have I ever heard a **BOO**.

Though I have something similar . . .

why don't you try my MOO?"

Then Little Ghost heard
what sounded like a **BOO!**

She flew a little closer . . .
then knew it was a MOO!

Little Ghost was sad, as up and off she flew,

heading for her home—without her precious **BOO**.

She'd asked all her friends and she'd looked everywhere.

She knew without a **BOO** there was no one she could **SCARE**.

"I'm sorry, Little Ghost, but I can't help you.
I've only just got up as the day is really new,
and I'm about to wake the world with a COCK-A-DOODLE-DOO.
Why don't you join me—and you can try it too?"

COCK-A-

"Thank you, Rooster, it's perfect for you,
but it's just not as scary as my **GHOSTLY BOO.**"

"Oh, hello, Rooster,
it's nice to see you.
I wonder, can you help me?
I'm looking for my **BOO**."

As the first light of day began to show,
the tiny ghost heard a rooster crow.

COCK-A-DOODLE-DOO!

"Thank you, Pigeon, it's perfect for you,
but it's just not as scary as my **GHOSTLY BOO.**"

"I'm sorry, Little Ghost, but I can't help you.
I woke up extra early to enjoy the starry view,
and while I was looking, I didn't hear a **BOO**.
Would you like to borrow my own gentle coo?"

Coo!
Coo!
Coo!

It was not a boo,
but a gentle coo.

"Oh, hello, Pigeon,
I'm glad it's you.
I wonder, can you help me?
I'm looking for my **BOO**."

From far above came a noise in a tree.
"That's my **BOO!** It belongs to me."

Coo!
Coo!

"Thank you, Owl. It's perfect for you,
but it's just not as scary as my **GHOSTLY BOO.**"

Would you like to borrow my

WHOO!
WHOO!
WHOO!"

"I'm sorry, Little Ghost, but I can't help you.
I've been out all night, had a tasty bite or two,
and while I was hunting, I didn't hear a **BOO**.

"Oh Owl, it's you!
I wonder, can you help me?
I'm looking for my **BOO**."

It wasn't a **BOO**,
but a WHOO-WHOO-WHOO!
And down flew Owl.

"I'll find it," cried Little Ghost. Off she flew,
looking and listening for her **SCARY BOO**.
Then she heard a noise in the dark, dark trees.

"Can that be my **BOO**?
Oh, let it be, please!"

WHOO!
WHOO!

Mama Ghost said, "My poor little one!
It looks as though your fright nights are done."

"I've lost my **BOO!** I've lost my **BOO!**
Where has it gone? What will I do?"

She opened her mouth—
but her **BOO** wasn't there!
All that came out was a rush of cold air.

LITTLE GHOST went out in the middle of the night
and flew up to someone to give them a **FRIGHT**.
She got in position, arms up, all prepared,
"Wait for it, lady, you're going to be

SCARED . . ."